GA G
Adventure
Travel Guide

COMPILED BY KATHY STRAWN

A 2002–2003
Travel Guide and Activity Book
for Girls in Action

Woman's Missionary Union
P. O. Box 830010
Birmingham, AL 35283–0010

For more information, visit the WMU Web site at www.wmu.com or the GA Web site
at www.gapassport.com or call 1-800-968-7301.

Dewey Decimal Classification: 266.007
Subject Headings: GIRLS IN ACTION (WMU)
                    MISSIONS EDUCATION
                    MISSIONS ACTIVITIES

Cover design by Karen Dillard
Inside design by Freda Souter

The publishers have made every effort to ensure that the Web sites suggested for GAs
to visit are entirely appropriate as learning enrichment resources. GA leaders and
parents, please work with girls when they use the Internet and help them navigate
only to those sites you believe are suitable. Be aware that many Web sites contain
links to other sites that may not be suitable for children.

ISBN: 1-56309-596-3
W027105•0402•30M1

GA GLOBAL ADVENTURE TRAVEL GUIDE

Use this travel guide as your constant companion as you travel over the globe in Girls in Action® (GA®) this year. You can use it both during GA meetings and at home. For each month September 2002 through August 2003, you will find several pages in this travel guide related to your GA meetings and other GA activities. Each month, read the related pages and do the activities they suggest. Then, with an adult's help, find the Internet Web sites listed for that month so that you can learn and see even more. Be sure to use the pullout map included in this book each month too.

TRAVEL TIP: Never give out personal information online without your parents' permission. Your name, address, and phone number are private, and you should not give them out on the Internet.

Use this travel guide to record things you discover as you have fun learning about people and places during GA this year. This travel guide can be your scrapbook of memories from an awesome adventure!

Ginny and GinA GA will be your guides.

PASSPORT

This passport/travel guide belongs to

Name: _____

place photo here

Address: _____

Phone Number: _____
Email Address: _____
Birthday: _____
Church: _____
School: _____

globe goes here

3

Me . . .

(Glue a picture of yourself here.)

And My Friends

(Glue a picture of your friends
here or write their names.)

Your Map

There is a pullout map included in this book. You will need it during each month to mark places you are studying and find out interesting facts. Once you remove the map, be sure to keep it in a safe place so you can use it each time you need it.

On your map, find the names of the seven continents. Make a star beside the name of the continent where you live.

Get Ready

Before I start on my GA global adventure, I need to:

⚜ Find out when and where my GA group will meet each week.

⚜ Invite all my friends to come with me to GA.

⚜ Locate the places we will visit during the year on my pull-out map included in this book.

⚜ Get a current copy of *Discovery* or *GA World* magazine.

⚜ Get the WorldVenture book for my grade.

September

DESTINATION:
The GA Global Adventure

GA means

G _ _ _ _ _   _ _

A _ _ _ _ _

   Choose a picture from the pages at the back of this book. Choose a picture from the ones marked "My Choice." Glue it onto the world map (included in this book) to show where you live.

   Choose another picture from "My Choice." Glue or tape it on the map at a place you would like to visit.

Here is a picture of our GA meeting.

We meet on _____ at _____.

(day)   (time)

6

IT'S TIME TO PRAY!

Write or draw here a prayer request you heard during your GA meeting.

WE'RE OFF!

Pennsylvania/South Jersey

United States Prison Ministry

Costa Rica	Chicago
Bosnia	Uganda
The Past	My Part
Paraguay	Thailand

Christmas in August

Look through this travel guide. Find the places you will visit in GA this year. Then locate those places on your map.

7

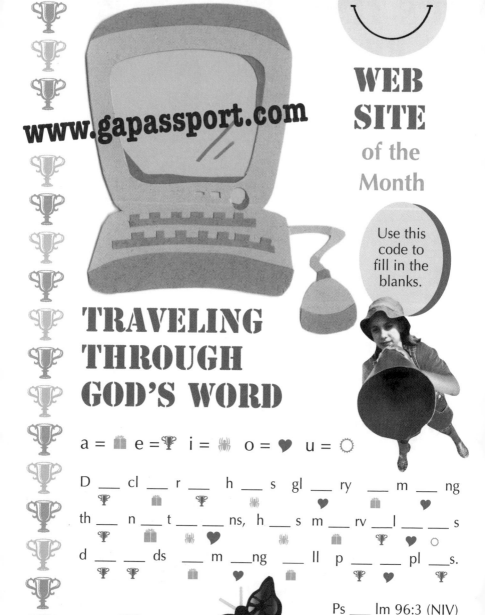

WEB SITE
of the Month

Use this code to fill in the blanks.

TRAVELING THROUGH GOD'S WORD

a = 🎁 e = 🏆 i = 🕷 o = ♥ u = ○

D __ cl __ r __ h __ s gl __ ry __ m __ ng
  🏆   🎁   🏆   🕷   ♥   🎁   ♥

th __ n __ t __ ns, h __ s m __ rv __ l __ __ s
  🏆   🎁 🕷♥   🕷   🎁   🏆 ♥ ○

d __ __ ds __ m __ ng __ ll p __ __ pl __ s.
 🏆 🏆   🎁   ♥   🎁   🏆 ♥   🏆

Ps __ lm 96:3 (NIV)
 🎁

8

DESTINATION: THAILAND

WEATHER CHART

The weather in Thailand today is (circle one):

full sun   rain   part sun   snow

TRAVELING THROUGH GOD'S WORD

From the pictures at the back of this book, cut out the picture of Thailand.
Glue or tape it here.

Hold this message up to a mirror and read it.

"We have a God who is close to us and answers our prayers"

(Deuteronomy 4:8 CEV).

9

ELEPHANT RIDES

Elephant rides are risky but fun. The rider sits way above the ground. You can see the scenery easily.

Elephants love water. So riders must be prepared to get wet! The elephants walk through rivers and sometimes spray their riders with the water.

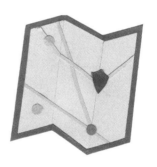

Use Your Map

Cut out the elephant picture from the pages at the back of this book. Glue or tape it to your map to mark Thailand.

Ministry

Take a picture of your GA group doing a ministry project. Glue or tape it here.

IMAGINE THAT!

- The durian grows in Thailand. It tastes like custard but smells like something rotten.
- Long ago elephants were used to carry soldiers during wars. Then they were used to carry big logs. Now they are mostly used to give rides to tourists.
- At the market, you might find meatballs, seafood, grasshoppers, scorpions, or even cockroaches to eat.
- *Krue toh* is an instrument made from a hollowed-out coconut with a piece of bamboo over it. The player beats the instrument with a stick to play it.

Speaking of . . .

Here are some useful phrases in Thai, a language of Thailand.

Excuse me—*Khaw thoht*
Yes—*Chai*
No—*Mai chai*
Thank you—*Khawp khun*
I don't know—*Mai roo*
Really/truly—*Jing jing*

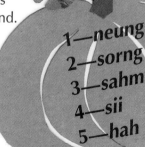

1—neung
2—sorng
3—sahm
4—sii
5—hah

DESTINATION: COSTA RICA

WEATHER CHART

The weather in Costa Rica today is (circle one):

full sun   rain   part sun   snow

Cut the shape of Costa Rica
from the pictures at the back
of this book. Glue or tape
the picture here.

TRAVELING THROUGH GOD'S WORD

What three things does Psalm 105:1 (TEV) tell us to do?

1. Give _____ to the Lord.

2. _____ His greatness.

3. _____ the nations what He has done.

13

IT'S TIME TO PRAY!

WEB SITE
of the Month

In each balloon, write a prayer request of missionaries in Costa Rica. Pray for each request.

www.google.com
(Click on Web Directory; then click on Regional; then click on Central America.)

14

```
flower middle  cut 1
```

TISSUE-PAPER FLOWERS

Costa Rica has many beautiful flowers. Try making some brightly colored tissue-paper flowers to remind you to pray for the people of Costa Rica.

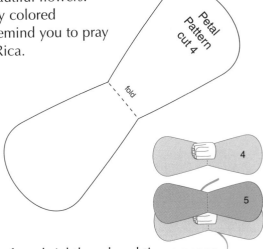

Petal
Pattern
cut 4

fold

You need:

yellow tissue paper
other brightly colored
  tissue paper
fine wire or chenille
  stem
scissors

To do:

1. Cut four petal patterns from brightly colored tissue paper.
2. Cut the flower middle from yellow paper. Snip along one edge.
3. Roll the flower middle into a bundle.
4. Place the bundle in the middle of the first petal.
5. Lay the second petal on top.
6. Place the third and fourth petals on the sides.
7. Pinch the center of all four petals. Twist the wire or chenille stem around the center.
8. Fold up the bottom petals to the top.

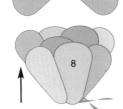

4

5

6 & 7

8

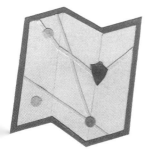

Use Your Map

Costa Rica is located in Central America between North America and South America. Look on your map just below Mexico. When you find Costa Rica, color it in with green to show that Costa Rica is a country with lots of trees and bushes.

THE FRUIT'S THE THING

The people of Costa Rica can get lots of fresh fruit. Make a fruit salad your family can enjoy. Tell them what you have learned about Costa Rica.

ENSALADA DE FRUTA (Fruit Salad)

Get any of these fruits:
bananas
pineapple
mangoes
guavas

Cut the fruit into chunks. Mix up the chunks. Serve.

Speaking of . . .

People in Costa Rica speak Spanish. Here are some helpful Spanish phrases to use in Costa Rica.

Excuse me—*Discúlpeme*
Yes—*Sí*
No—*No*
Thank you—*Gracias*
I don't know—*No se*

1—*uno*
2—*dos*
3—*tres*
4—*cuatro*
5—*cinco*

DESTINATION: BOSNIA

Weather Chart   Today the weather in Bosnia is (circle one):

| full sun | rain | part sun | snow |

From the pictures at the back of this book, cut out the shape of Bosnia. Glue or tape it here.

TRAVELING THROUGH GOD'S WORD

The letters of Ephesians 4:32 (TEV) got squeezed together. Draw a line between each word. Use your Bible if you need help.

Bekindandtenderheartedtoone anotherandforgiveoneanotheras GodhasforgivenyouthroughChrist.

17

IT'S TIME TO PRAY!

In the Christmas ornament, write or draw a prayer for the people of Bosnia and the missionaries working there.

After you pray, cut out a Christmas present from the back of this book and glue or tape it here.

WEB SITE
of the Month

www.bosnet.org
/bosnia/culture/food.shtml

UM, UM, GOOD

Bosnians like to eat pizza, but it is slightly different from American pizza. It often has a cooked egg in the middle.

Bosnian hotpot stew is a slow-cooked mixture of layers of meat (such as lamb or beef) and vegetables (such as onions, peppers, or potatoes).

Want to make a Bosnian food?
Just fill pita bread with meat or vegetables!

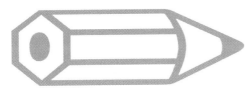

Use Your Map

Spread out your map. See if you can find Bosnia. If you were to travel to Bosnia, how do you think you would go? How long do you think it would take to get there?

19

THE LOTTIE MOON
CHRISTMAS OFFERING
for International Missions

In December, Baptists gather money especially to help people in other countries learn about Jesus. Will you help? Color one of the lights red for each dime you give. Color a light blue for each quarter and a light green for each dollar you give. Add more lights if you need them!

If I could give a gift to the children in Bosnia, this is what I would give.

DESTINATION:
UNITED STATES
PRISON MINISTRY

Circle in blue the weather picture for today's weather in Sparta, Missouri.

Weather Chart Circle in red the weather picture for today's weather in Richmond, Virginia.

full sun   rain   part sun   snow

From the pictures at the back of this book, cut out the shapes of Virginia and Missouri. Glue or tape them here.

TRAVELING THROUGH
GOD'S WORD

Number these phrases of Matthew 25:36*b* (TEV) in order.

and you took

care of me,

I was sick

in prison

me.

and you visited

IT'S TIME TO PRAY!

Choose a time you will pray for prisoners and their families. Draw that time on the clock.

After you have prayed, cut out the clock picture from the back of this book.

Glue or tape it here.

Use Your Map

Color in the states of Virginia and Missouri on your map. If you live in Virginia or Missouri, add a smiley face too. The missionaries you study at GA during January work in Virginia and Missouri.

www.gapassport.com
www.wmu.com

WEB SITES
of the Month

I WOULD MISS . . .

What would you miss most if you were in prison? Write or draw your list on the snowman.

Attach here a photo or a drawing of what you did.

WE DID IT!

What did you do for a ministry project this month?

From the pictures at the back of this book, find those of items for prison ministry kits. Cut out the pictures and glue or tape them onto this kit.

PRISON MINISTRY KITS

ENCOURAGEMENT

Which four of these words mean encourage?

cheer

urge

warn

support

sadden

assure

How could you encourage a friend whose family member is in jail? Talk with other GAs about ways to encourage.

24

February

DESTINATION: MY PART

My Part in Ministry

Sometimes you do ministry projects with other GAs. Did you know you can do ministry projects on your own? Here are ideas of some you can do alone.

- Record yourself reading a book on tape. Donate the book and tape to a hospital or shelter.
- Design a "Thinking of You" card. Give the card to someone who needs a friend.
- Arrange a plate of cookies and take them to a neighbor. What others can you add? Always be sure to tell people that God loves them!

YIELD

EXIT

Place an "I Can" picture from the back of this book beside one ministry project you can do.

TRAVELING THROUGH GOD'S WORD

Fill in these blanks of Proverbs 3:6 (TEV).

"Remember the _____ in _____ you

do, and he will_____ you the right _____."

SCHOOL ZONE 55 SLOW YIELD STOP

Doing my part means praying. Use the sentence starters on the handprint below to help you pray for missions.

I ♥ CAN PRAY

Thank You, God, for . . .

Please help missionaries to . . .

I pray especially for the people who live in . . .

One thing I ask You to help missionaries do is . . .

Place an "I Can" picture on the hand after you pray. (See the pictures at the back of this book.)

Dear God, . . .

Please help me to be like a missionary by . . .

I CAN GIVE

When GAs give money to missions offerings, they are doing their part. Add pictures from the back of this book to the cupcakes to show what your offerings can buy.

$5.00
Set of seven Bible-story videotapes in Vietnam

$1.00
Songbook in Malawi

$10.00
CD-ROM library of study tools for a church among Arab peoples

WEB SITE
of the Month

www.imb.org/pray

27

DESTINATION:
MULTIFAMILY HOUSING IN PENNSYLVANIA/SOUTH JERSEY

Weather Chart
The weather today in Pennsylvania/South Jersey is (circle one):

full sun   rain   part sun   snow

Cut out the Pennsylvania/South Jersey shape from the back of this book. Glue or tape it here.

TRAVELING THROUGH GOD'S WORD

Connect the words of Luke 10:5 (TEV) in the correct order.

What did you make?

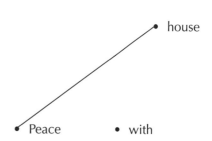

• be

this •   • house

• Peace   • with

IT'S TIME TO PRAY!

Prayer Request

One good thing about living in multifamily housing is . . .

Missionary's Name

Missionary's Name

Fill in the information using *Discovery* and *GA World*. Pray for the missionaries and the request.

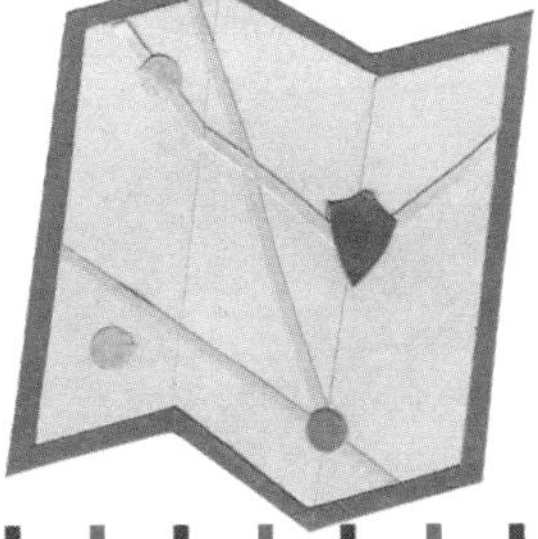

Use Your Map

Find Pennsylvania/South Jersey on your map. Glue or tape a picture of an apartment building at the spot. (The picture is at the back of this book.)

ALIKE AND DIFFERENT

Houses come in many
shapes and sizes.
Draw your house here
or take a photo and attach it here.

How is your house like other houses?

How is your house different from
other houses?

INDOOR GAMES

Often children who live in multifamily housing have limited space for playing outdoors. But lots of games can be played indoors. Here's one.

I Spy

Sit in the middle of a room. Without getting up, try to see or to "spy" things in the room that begin with each letter of the alphabet. Start with *A* and try to go all the way to *Z*. This game can be played alone or with friends.

WEB SITE
of the Month
www.habitat.org
Habitat for Humanity builds homes for people who need them.

DESTINATION:
DETOUR TO THE PAST

Then and Now

Annie Armstrong probably rode one of these.

Nannie Helen Burroughs may have ridden in one of these.

In which of these have you ridden?

Hairstyles change from year to year. To find out how you might have looked in the early 1900s, cut out the face in one of your school photos. Put your face in this space.

How do you like what you see?

Annie Armstrong and Nannie H. Burroughs would have worn clothes much like this.

From the pictures at the back of this book, pick pictures of clothing you like to wear. Tape or glue them here.

Ministry

Pretend you are writing a postcard to a friend. Tell your friend what your GA group did for a ministry project this month.

Place Stamp Here

IT'S TIME TO PRAY!

The Past
Thank God for people like Annie Armstrong and Nannie H. Burroughs who went before you.

The Future
Ask God to help you know what He wants you to do and to help you to do it.

The Present
Ask God to especially bless missionaries who have birthdays today.

Use Your Map
Annie Armstrong was born in the state of Maryland. Color in Maryland on your map.

TRAVELING THROUGH GOD'S WORD

Finish each letter to find the words of Psalm 37:5 (CEV).

Let the Lord lead you and trust him to help.

DESTINATION: PARAGUAY

Weather Chart

Today the weather in Paraguay is (circle one):

full sun   rain   part sun   snow

TRAVELING THROUGH GOD'S WORD

Cut out the shape of Paraguay from the pictures at the back of this book.

Glue or tape it here.

Use the code on the flowers to write the beginning of Romans 15:7 (TEV).

___ ___ ___ ___ ___ ___
1   2   2   3   7   9

___ ___ ___ ___ ___ ___ ___ ___ ___ ___
6   5   3   1   5   6   9   4   3   8

Can you finish the verse on your own?

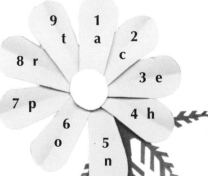

9 t   1 a   2 c
8 r   3 e
7 p   4 h
6 o   5 n

35

IT'S TIME TO PRAY!

Pray for the safety of missionaries in Paraguay. Pray that the people of Paraguay will listen to the good news of Jesus. When you finish, cut out the flag of Paraguay from the back of this book
Glue or tape it
to the suitcase.

WEB SITE
of the Month

www.mrdowling.com
(Click on South America.)

EL RELOJ OR THE CLOCK

This jump rope game is played all over South America. Why do you think it is called "the clock"?

Get a long rope. Choose two players to start turning the rope for jumping. The other players line up to take turns jumping.

The first player runs through without jumping or touching the rope. The next player runs in, jumps once, and runs out. The next player jumps twice and so on until a player jumps 12 times.

If anyone misses a jump or counts the wrong number, she takes a turn turning the rope and the game begins again.

Use Your Map

Find Paraguay on your map. Color it in. Follow the arrow from Paraguay to an interesting fact about the country.

FIESTA TIME

Decorations: Straw hats, bright hand-kerchiefs, tissue-paper flowers (see "Destination: Costa Rica" in this book for ways to make the flowers.)

Food: Citrus fruits
     (especially oranges)
     Beef stew
     Tea to drink

Games: Play "the clock"
(p. 37 of this book).

The people of Paraguay love fiestas, or parties. Plan and have your own fiesta with other GAs or with your family.

Speaking of . . .

Paraguay has two official languages: Spanish and Guaraní. Many people speak both languages. More people speak Guaraní than speak Spanish.

Mba'exipá [mbaa-ay-she-pa]—How are you?
Iporá [e-pour-rah]—Nice, pretty, good
Cuñatai [koon-ya-tai-eé]—Girl

Which language do you think would be easier to learn: Spanish or Guaraní?

38

DESTINATION:
THE CITY—CHICAGO

Weather Chart   The weather today in Chicago is (circle one):

full sun   rain   part sun   snow

What state is Chicago in? Cut out that state's
shape from the back of the book. Tape it here.

(Hint: The
state has the
same shape
as this out-
line.)

TRAVELING
THROUGH
GOD'S
WORD

Write the
correct vowel in
each blank to
complete Romans
10:12b (TEV).

"G __ d __ s th __ s __ m __ L __ rd

__ f __ ll __ nd r __ chl __ bl __ ss __ s __ ll wh __

c __ ll t __ h __ m."   **Use your Bible if you need help.**

39

IT'S TIME TO PRAY!

Write on the hot dog a prayer for people who live in Chicago.

Remember Chicago has rich people, poor people, international people, and homeless people.

WEB SITE of the Month

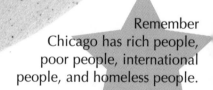

www.chicago.il. org/FACTS.HTM

FAST FACTS

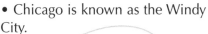

- Chicago is known as the Windy City.
- The first ferris wheel was introduced in Chicago at the World's Columbian Exposition in 1893.
- The world's largest gum manufacturer, William Wrigley, Jr. Company, is located in Chicago. It produces more than 20 million packages of gum a day.
- The first cafeteria was in Chicago.
  - Cracker Jack and Schwinn bicycles got their starts in Chicago.

Use Your Map

Get a long string (about three feet). Hold one end of the string at Chicago on the map. Stretch the string to Japan. Hold that place on the string. Now stretch the string from Chicago to England. Which one is further from Chicago? Choose a picture from "My Choice" at the back of this book. Put it on the country that is furthest from Chicago.

Try these two: Mexico City or Hawaii
               Singapore or Paraguay

CHICAGO-STYLE PIZZA

Chicago is serious about pizza.

A favorite is deep-dish pizza. If you want to make your own Chicago-style pizza at home, use a 10-inch cake pan instead of a pizza pan or a cookie sheet. Lay the dough in the pan and stretch it to the edges. Be sure to build up the edge to hold the filling. Add your favorite pizza filling and bake in a 500°F oven about 15 minutes. Reduce heat to 400°F and bake an additional 10 minutes.

What Do You Know?

• The Tribune Tower in Chicago has outer walls with pieces from famous buildings around the world. Some of those buildings are the Alamo, the Great Pyramid (Egypt), Westminster Abbey (London), Hamlet's Castle, the Taj Mahal, and Fort Sumter.
• The Wrigley Building was designed to look like a luscious birthday cake!

DESTINATION: UGANDA

Weather Chart   Today's weather in Uganda is (circle one):

full sun   rain   part sun   snow

From the pictures at the back of this book, find the shape of Uganda. Cut it out. Tape or glue it here.

TRAVELING THROUGH GOD'S WORD

"My children, our love should not be just words and talk; it must be true love, which shows itself in action" 1 John 3:18 (TEV).

Draw one way you can obey 1 John 3:18.

IT'S TIME TO PRAY!

Use *Discovery* or *GA World* to find prayer requests about Uganda's people and missionaries there. Write a request or a missionary's name on each firecracker.

www.ipl.org/youth
(Click on Our World;
then click on
Geography
& World Culture.)

WEB SITE
of the
Month

GORILLA RULES

Mountain gorillas, the world's most endangered ape, are found in southwest Uganda.

Only six visitors may visit a group of gorillas in their habitat each day. Visitors must obey strict rules.

• Keep your voices low.

• Wash your hands before going out to see the gorillas.

• Stay 15 feet away from the gorillas.

• Stay in a tight group.

• If a gorilla charges, crouch down slowly. Do not look the gorilla in the eye. Wait for the gorilla to pass. Do not run away.

Visitors must wash their hands and stay apart from the gorillas to keep them from catching sickness from humans.

Use Your Map

Find Uganda on your map. On what continent is it located?

Tape or glue a gorilla picture from the back of this book near Uganda on your map.

MINISTRY

Write or draw here what your GA group did for a ministry project this month.

Speaking of . . .

Swahili is spoken in many parts of Uganda.

Please—*Tafadhali*
Thank you—*Asante*
Hello (to one person)
—*Jambo*
No—*Katu*
Yes (used by females)
—*Bee!*

DESTINATION:
CHRISTMAS IN AUGUST

Pray for hospital chaplains who will receive Christmas-in-August gifts to give away.

Pray for prisoners who will get Christmas-in-August gifts.

Pray for people in Baptist centers who will be helped by the Christmas-in-August gifts they get.

TRAVELING THROUGH GOD'S WORD

Follow the lines to find the correct letters to print in the boxes.

G□d lov□s the □ne wh□ □iv□s □ladly.

2 Corinthians 9:7 (TEV)

TRIM THE TREE

Find in the pictures at the back of this book items to be given for Christmas-in-August gifts. Glue or tape them onto the Christmas tree.

Use Your Map

The very first Christmas-in-August gifts were sent to China. Cut from the pictures at the back of this book a Christmas wreath. Glue or tape it to China on the map.

Notice how far China is from where you live.

Weather Chart The weather today where I live is (circle one):

full sun   rain   part sun   snow

Now make a red circle around the picture of weather you usually have at Christmas.

WEB SITE
of the Month

www.gapassport.com
www.4kidz.com

CHRISTMAS FUN FACTS

Fireworks are a big part of Christmas celebrations in China.

In Italy, many families eat no food at all on Christmas Eve. Then they enjoy a huge feast on Christmas Day.

In Holland, children put out wooden shoes at Christmastime much like some people hang stockings.

In Ghana, Christmas celebrations last for eight days.

In Hawaii, part of the United States, many people eat baked bananas. Try one yourself!

Wash a banana. Do not peel it.
Place the banana in a pan with enough water to cover the bottom of the pan.
Bake at 350°F for 30–45 minutes, until the banana is soft.
Eat with butter, salt, and pepper.

SPEAKING OF . . .

People all around the world celebrate Christmas.
Here are some of their Christmas greetings:
Mexico—*Feliz Navidad*
England—Happy Christmas
Sweden—*God Jul*
China—*Sheng Tan Kuai Loh*
Brazil—*Felize Natal*

Countries and States

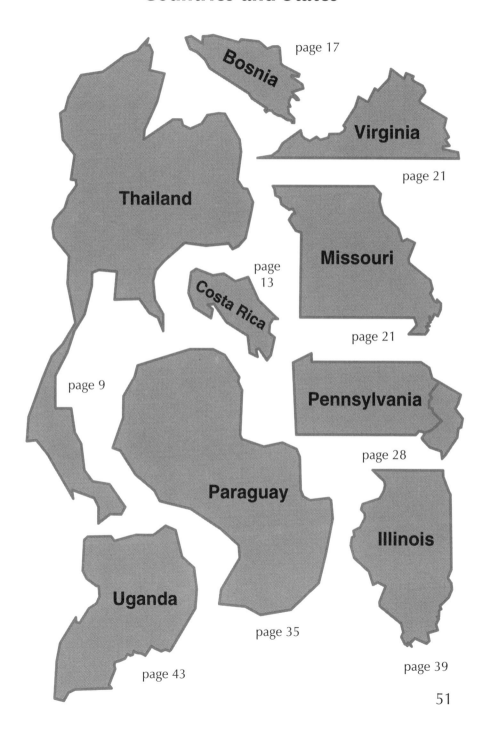

Bosnia page 17

Virginia page 21

Thailand

Missouri

page 13

Costa Rica

page 21

page 9

Pennsylvania

page 28

Paraguay

Illinois

Uganda

page 35

page 43

page 39

Christmas in August

map (see page 49)

page 25

Bible

Shampoo
Herbal Shampoo

SOAP

page 48

page 18

map
(see page 45)

page 22

page 3

map
(see page 11)

page 24

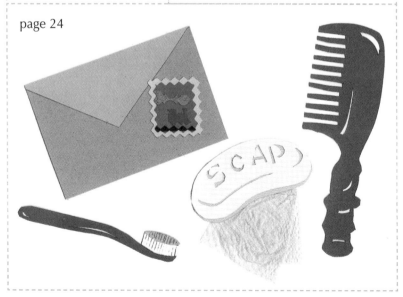

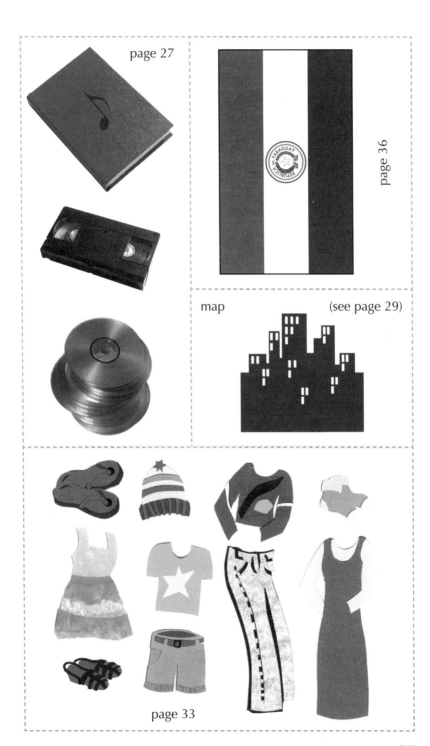

page 27

page 36

map (see page 29)

page 33

Glue or tape these to pages in
months when you did them.

59

My Choice
Use these anywhere in your book or on your map.

THE BEST
OF MY GA TRIP

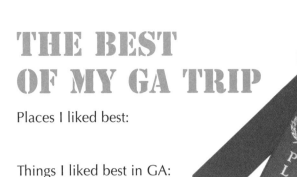

Places I liked best:

Things I liked best in GA:

People I've learned about:

Tips for Making a Trip Go Faster

1. Say, "Quick trip tips" three times— fast. What other tongue twisters do you know?
2. Make as many words as possible using only the letters in your name.
3. Do a sign search. Count how many hospital signs, airport signs, one-way signs, and speed limit signs you see.
4. Ask grown-ups to tell about trips they took when they were young.
5. Have a magazine alphabet hunt. Look in a magazine to find items that start with each letter of the alphabet.

63